HOW TO DRAW
CATS

Lucy Smith

Designed by Fiona Brown

Illustrated by
Chris Chapman

Additional designs by Iain Ashman
Additional illustrations by Derick Bown
Cartoon illustrations by Jo Wright

Contents

About this book

Cats make wonderful pictures with their sleek bodies, beautiful markings and graceful, nimble movements. This book shows you how to draw all sorts, from tiny kittens to fierce tigers.

Pages 10-15 show some typical cat moods and action poses.

Wild cats are on pages 20-23 and 31.

Because cats spend a lot of time on the move, they are a challenge to draw well. Copying the pictures in this book will help you practise.

The copying method at the bottom of the page is a good way to start. It works for any picture.

For kittens, see pages 18-19.

Copy cats

Tape the top edge of the overlay down with masking tape, which lifts off without tearing.

Look for the shapes shown in red first, then the green, then the blue.

Flip up the overlay to check any details that are unclear.

Cats may look hard to draw, but you can break them down into simple shapes. Try this copying technique. It is better than tracing a picture because it helps you understand how a cat's body is made up.

Lay a sheet of tracing paper over the picture and fasten it as shown. Looking through it, try to pick out basic shapes that make up the cat's body. Draw them on the tracing paper overlay with a soft pencil.*

*Any pencil coded HB, 1B, 2B, 3B, 4B or 5B will do.

Sketching cats from life

Try to do light, flowing strokes first. You can strengthen the lines when you think they look right.

Sketch parts, as well as the whole cat.

Look closely at how the body is stretched or curved, at the angle of the head and the position of the legs and tail.

Use soft pencils for quick lines.

Sketching live cats is a good way to practise watching and drawing them. As you sketch, don't stop to rub things out; work on getting the main lines right and keeping your strokes flowing. You can put more detail in later.

You could sketch wild or big cats (see pages 20-23) at a zoo or safari park. If you have a video recorder, try taping a TV programme about them. Replay it and use the "pause" button to freeze the action while you sketch the animals.

Once you have worked out the basic shapes, you can make them bigger or smaller to change the size of the cat.

When you have done the outline, rub out the basic shapes.

Take the overlay off the original picture. Tidy up the outline, referring to the original for help. You can either add details and colour on the overlay, or retrace the outline on thicker paper first.

Try copying this tiger using the method on the left and the shapes shown above right.

3

What to look for

This picture shows the main points to look for when drawing a cat. As you draw, it helps to think of the cat as made up mostly of simple, rounded shapes. Try to use smooth, curving lines to bring out its graceful build.

The head is quite small compared with the body. It is held high and forward, which helps the cat to see and smell its prey when it hunts. The skull is fairly broad and rounded on top.

The spine is long and so supple that the cat can arch its back nearly double without hurting itself.

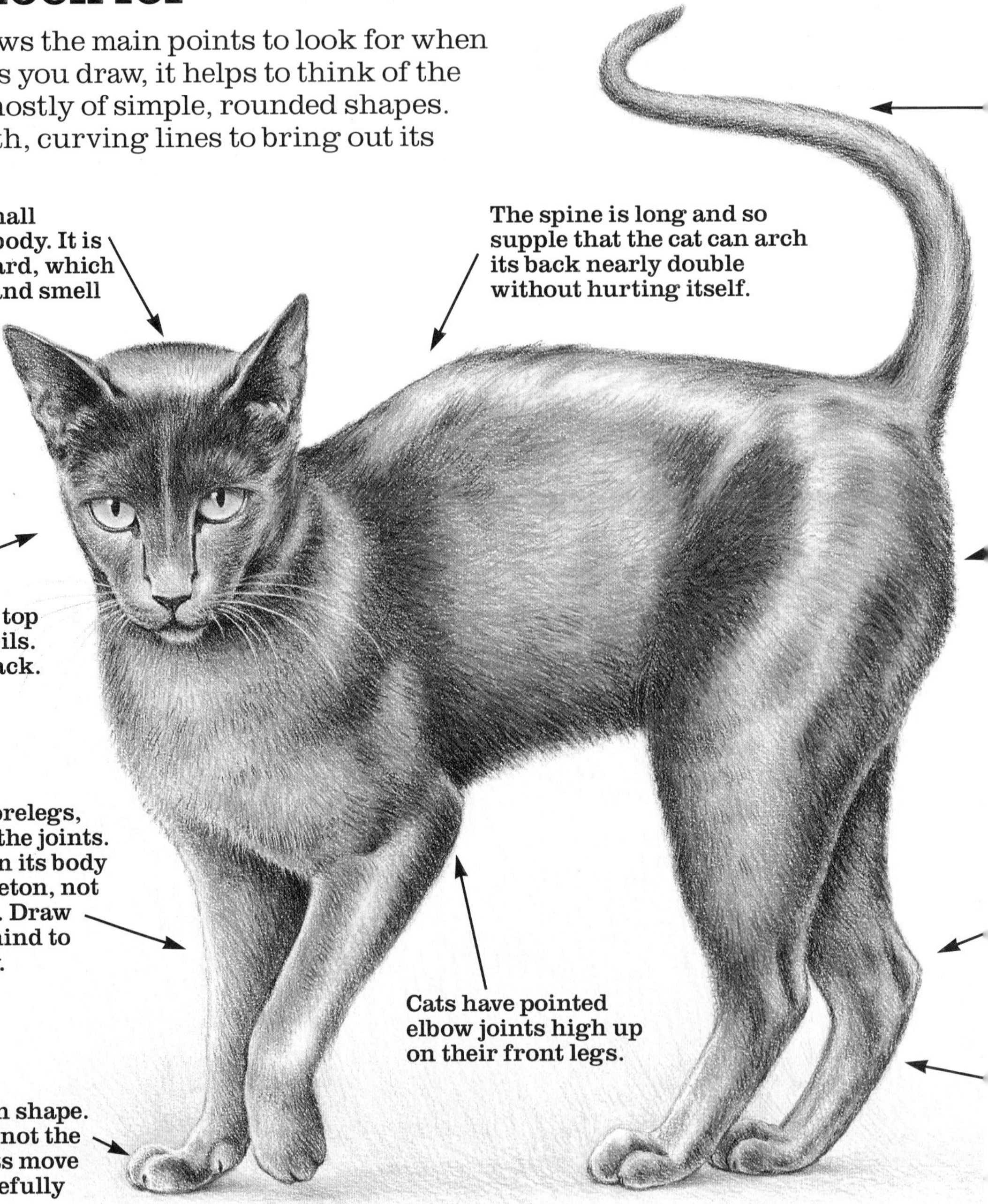

Colour the eyes yellowy-green. Add darker green at the top and around the pupils. Make these solid black.

The front legs, or forelegs, are very flexible at the joints. All the cat's legs join its body high up on the skeleton, not just at tummy level. Draw them with this in mind to make the lines flow.

Cats have pointed elbow joints high up on their front legs.

The paws are oval in shape. They are only toes, not the cat's whole feet. Cats move so lightly and gracefully because they balance on their toes.

Most cats have tails almost as long and supple as their spines. The tail is really an extension of the spine, so try to make the two flow in a continuous line.

The hips or hindquarters are very muscular, which is why cats can spring so far and fast. You can find out how to make them look muscular below.

These pointed joints are the cat's heels, called hocks. They stick out backwards when it is standing up, but rest on the ground when it sits.

The muscles under the skin make the curves you see on the surface. You can make a short-haired cat like this look muscular by shading faint lines in a darker colour.

Drawing the cat

Using a soft pencil, draw the big ovals of the body, chest and hindquarters first, and the smaller head circle. Add the legs, paws and tail, then the face and ears.*

The line of the cat's belly is almost straight.

The legs join the body high up.

Refine the shapes to get the cat's outline. Apply pale grey-blue as a base. Let the paper show through on the lightest parts to give a sheen to the fur.

Use colour pencil or watercolour wash for the base.

Add detail to the face*: colouring the eyes helps bring it to life. Darker grey shadows give the cat form (see the tips on the right).

✏ Professional tips

Proportions. To help you get the proportions and outline right, look at the space in between parts of the cat: for example, the shape of the space framed by the cat's tummy and legs, and the space between its hindlegs.

Shadows. Adding shadows to your drawing helps to make the cat look three-dimensional and rounded. You need to shade the parts which the light does not fall on directly.

It helps to imagine the cat's body as a cylinder.

Direction of light.

Direction of light.

Mark arrows on your drawing to show the direction of the light. This helps you work out which parts of the cat should be in shadow.

*You can find out how to draw a cat's face in detail on pages 6-7.

Drawing the head and face

Cats use all their facial features in many ways to show their moods, so drawing the face well adds character and life to your pictures. Here you can see how to structure the head. Opposite are more hints about how to draw the cat's main features in detail to get a really convincing look.

A cat's head

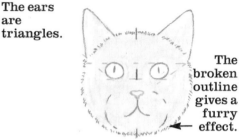

Horizontal lines make sure the eyes are level. →

The ears are triangles.

Use a soft pencil.

The broken outline gives a furry effect.

Draw a circle. Do a vertical line down the middle to help you position the features evenly on each side of the face. Add a small oval in the lower part of the circle for the muzzle.

Near the top of the oval, draw a little upside-down triangle for the nose. Draw wedge shapes out from this to the rim of the head circle to help you place the eyes and ears as shown.

Add the mouth as an upside-down Y-shape. Rub out the construction lines. Colour the head pale fawn, fanning your pencil or brush strokes out from the middle to follow the lie of the fur.

Shade under and around the muzzle to help bring it out from the face. Refine the outlines and add detail to all the features (see below and opposite).

To colour the eyes, do a layer of yellow, then orange. Add brown shadows. If you use paint, let each layer dry before applying the next. Do black pupils.

← The ears sit high on the head, far apart, helping the cat to hear well. →

Add tan shadows. →

The mouth is small when shut, with very fine lips.

The eyes are big and widely spaced.

The nose and eyes together form a V-shape.

Draw the whiskers last, in white.

Eyes

The most striking things about a cat's face are its eyes. They give an immediate impression of its character. Here is some help with making them look alive.

The eyes are spheres so the highlight falls in the same place on each one.

You can make the eyes look more intense and realistic by colouring them darker at the top and lighter towards the bottom. Adding a white highlight to each eye makes it look bright and luminous.

In dim light, the pupil* widens and is circular, filling most of the eye.

In good light, it is a medium-sized vertical oval.

In strong light, it becomes a narrow slit.

Cats' pupils change size and shape depending on how much light there is. This helps the cat to see better.

Nose

The nose is small with a triangular, hairless tip called the "nose leather". This is very sensitive to touch, so cats use it to examine things.

Do the nostrils darker to make them look hollow.

Do tiny dots of colour very close together to build up a textured effect on the nose leather. This technique is called stippling.**

Whiskers

The whiskers are extremely sensitive. The cat uses them to touch things and to sense changes in the air around it.

Do a few single whiskers above the eyes.

Do little dots where each whisker grows.

Most of the whiskers grow in several rows on each side of the muzzle. They twitch, bristle or flatten depending on how the cat feels. They are usually white.

Ears

Cats' ears can pick up the tiniest squeak of a mouse or chirp of a bird. They are quite big and cone-shaped so they catch sounds easily.

A cross-section of a cat's ear, seen from the side.

The ear is like half a cone, turned upside-down.

Each ear can twitch separately sideways, back or forwards to focus on where a sound is coming from.

Do longer, lighter hairs here.

Shading along the outer edge makes the ear look three-dimensional.

Cats often have longer hairs along the inner edge of each ear. Inside, the ear has little or no fur, so the skin is paler. Do the innermost bit darker though to give it shape.

*The pupil is the dark bit in the middle of the eye.
**See page 9.

Fur and markings

The only parts of a cat's body not covered with fur are the tip of its nose and its paw-pads, so it is worth practising drawing fur in detail to get a life-like effect. Here you can see ways to do the main types.

Drawing different types of fur

For short fur, pick out the palest colour in the coat and apply it in either light pencil or a watercolour wash (see opposite). When it is dry, add lots of short, close strokes of darker colour.*

Colour long fur in the same way as short, but use longer, looser strokes. Group several strokes together as shown to get a tufted effect. Make them flow down rather than along the sides of the body.

Rex cats (see page 17) have curly fur. To draw it, do short, arched strokes very close together in rows over the base colour. Let this show through in between the rows for a rippling, shiny look.

Common colours and markings

Tabby cats have pale coats with dark stripes. Start by applying the base colour. When it is dry, add the stripes. Make them follow the curves of the cat's body (see pages 12 and 19).

To draw a white cat on pale paper, use coloured shading to give it shape. Try warm fawns or yellows to get a sunlit or firelit effect, or cool blues if the cat is in moonlight or shadow.

For cats with white patches, colour the darker areas of the coat first, letting some white show around the edges where the dark and light hairs overlap. Then add soft shading on the white parts.

Make your strokes follow the direction of the fur, pointing along the body.

Techniques and materials

Below are examples of different drawing methods and materials which create convincing furry effects. Use a sharp pencil or fine brush to draw single hairs.

Coloured pencils

Hatching is lots of short, straight lines done side by side close together. It is good for short, sleek fur.

Cross-hatching is layers of short lines going in different directions. It gives a dark, dense look, useful for shadows.

Blocking means using the side of the pencil point to get a flat area of colour with no gaps showing.

Coloured pencils used on a rough-textured paper give a broken, fuzzy line which is good for fluffy or long fur.

On hard paper, scratch through coloured pencil or wax crayon with a sharp compass point to do fine white hairs.

Watercolours

The damp paper helps the colour blend in and gives a more even tone.

A watercolour wash is a quick way to do the first layer of colour. First mix the paint. With a soft, thickish brush, wet the paper with water. When it has soaked in but is still damp, put plenty of colour on the brush. Starting at the top of the page, do bold, quick strokes to and fro ◄ until you reach the bottom.

Stippling. With a small, blunt brush, do masses of tiny dots of colour close together. A stiff brush works well, or cut the tip ◄ off a soft one.

Stiff brush

Soft brush

◄ For fine detail, dab a tiny amount of paint on a brush and apply it in strokes over a dry wash. This method is called "dry brush".

◄ Wet watercolour. Apply paint to a wet paper or wash to get a blurred, soft effect which is good for drawing realistic-looking markings.

9

Moods and expressions

Cats are very expressive and use their whole bodies to show how they feel. These two pages show some typical moods to draw, and give you tips on how to make them look really vivid.

Do the red shapes first, then the green, then the blue.

Do triangles for the ears.

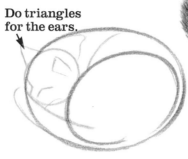

The eyes are slanting slits when shut.

A curved, furry outline gives a peaceful, cosy look.

Sleepy

A cat curled up snugly like this in a ball is a fairly easy subject to draw, because the whole picture makes an oval shape.

In pencil, do the basic shapes as shown. Refine the outlines, then build up the tabby markings using the method on page 8. Use

pastels or watercolours to get a soft, gentle feel. A pinky haze around the cat and orange highlights on its fur suggest a fireside glow.

Aggressive

The tail is up and the back is arched.

The ears are back and out.

The hips are tucked under, ready to spring.

One front paw is poised to lash out.

Short, sharp strokes here make the fur look bristly.

The cat stands sideways with its fur out to look bigger.

Whiskers held up, forwards and out exaggerate the snarl.

Add the teeth in white poster paint when the other colours are dry.

Claws out.

A threatened cat may react aggressively like this. As you do the basic shapes, note how this pose makes the cat look as big as possible.

Go over the outlines, making them bold and strong to suggest the fierce mood and add impact to the picture. Apply pale fawn as a base.

This mottled coat pattern is called tortoiseshell. Build it up by adding patches of gold, rust, dark brown and black once the base is dry.

Alert

Because you are seeing this cat almost head on, you need to draw the parts nearest to you bigger than the rest. To make the front and back legs look as if they are lined up behind each other, close the gaps between them. This is called foreshortening.*
To get this pose right, trace the basic body shapes carefully.

The cat is upright with its head and tail held high.

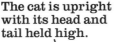

The head looks big as it is nearest.

The body ovals overlap to bring the front and back legs close together.

Bold shapes make the drawing look lively.

The tail is curved up like a question mark.

Ears pricked.

Eyes wide.

The back legs are drawn shorter than the front so they seem further away.

This gap is shorter than in a side view.

Frightened

Try to work out the basic shapes of this frightened cat for yourself. Its whole body is tense and crouching back as it cowers away in terror.

Arched back.

Ears flat.

Head down.

For spiky fur, draw short, straight lines out from the middle of the body.

Chin in.

Curved tail.

Legs bent.

*There is more about foreshortening on page 15.

Relaxed

Try drawing this contented cat in white on black or dark paper. First work out the basic shapes and draw them in white pencil. Apply a thin wash of white watercolour paint all over. When it is dry, leave this layer to show through on the shadowy parts and build up the palest areas, or highlights, with white crayon.

Let the paper show through to mark the line of the chin.

Do long, loose lines for a supple look.

Add a patterned rug in coloured pencils to make an eye-catching background.

Cats in action

Cats are very agile, so drawing them in action is hard because they move fast and get into all sorts of acrobatic positions. Here is advice on getting a sense of movement into a drawing, as well as some action pictures to try.

Loping cat

Lengthen the neck.

The tail is up. →

Just do stick figures at this stage.

Draw some paws lifted to show the cat is in mid-stride.

Place the head further forward.

The upright ears and tail add a sprightly touch.

Tilt the body slightly.

The hind legs propel the cat forward.

Use soft pencil for speed.

Start with lots of quick, simple line sketches to try to get the basic position right. If the picture looks too static, as above, don't worry. Keep sketching until your lines start to flow. Exaggerating them a bit, as in this picture, can improve the sense of movement.

▲ Once the basic lines are right, put in the body shapes as shown. Use a soft pencil and don't press hard at this stage: keep the lines light and flowing.

Improve the outlines, making them stronger and cleaner now to give a feeling of energy. Rub out any unwanted marks before applying a fawn base.

Professional tip

Use the space around the cat to suggest movement, by keeping the background simple. A detailed one is distracting and slows the movement down by cluttering the picture and blurring the outlines.

The eyes fixed ahead give a purposeful look.

◄ Add shading as shown, then the russet stripes. Put in a couple of lines to show the ground level. This gives the raised paws an extra lift.

The curving and stretching stripes increase the sense of moving muscles.

12

Sharpening claws

The whole position forms a wide U-shape.

A deep bend here gives a strong pulling effect.

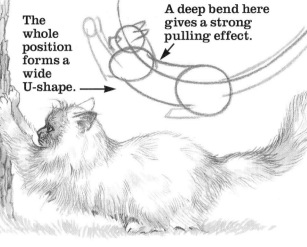

Washing

Cats have such supple spines that they can bend almost double, like this, to wash their hindquarters. This position looks hard to draw because it is so contorted, but the basic shapes are quite simple.

For this picture, draw the cat first. Start by doing a curving line as shown to get the feel of the movement sweeping through the whole body from toes to tail. This line will also help you position the basic shapes.

The hind legs are stretched out in a V-shape.

The spine is curved almost into a circle.

Fighting

Try copying this picture, using the method on pages 2-3 to discover the basic body shapes. The tips here will help you position the cats.

The cat's back is parallel with the dark cat's left foreleg.

The shape of the whole picture is like a wide upside-down triangle.

For this cat, use bold curves to show how its whole body is coiled and arched ready to spring forward.

This cat is protecting itself. Its body is off-balance and its legs and tail stretched taut.

There are more action pictures to try on the next two pages.

Springing down

The head is up, looking at where the cat aims to land.

To draw this springing cat, do a long oval for the main part of the body, which is stretched as the cat reaches down to reduce the distance it has to drop. Notice that the chest and thigh ovals are parallel, showing how the cat has balanced itself perfectly for the leap. Its back legs are folded ready to push it off into the air.

◀

Leaping

Cats can jump up to ▶ four or five times their own height. For this dynamic picture, draw the cat in the usual way. As you put in the shading*, add a shadow on the ground too. This is an easy but effective way of showing that the cat is high in the air.

A background of sky with no ground visible suggests the cat is high up and adds an element of risk to the picture.

The hind legs are long and taut. ➡

The tail is up and out to help the cat balance in the air.

Stretching

Cats nearly always stretch their whole bodies like this just after waking up. When you have drawn this cat, add a long, thin shadow under it as shown to increase the stretched look.

This smooth curve gives a supple feel.

The lifted forepaw gives a sense of movement.

14   *Siamese markings like these are described on page 16.*

Stalking

◀ Cats crouch down low like this to stalk their prey. You need to use foreshortening here because the cat is coming towards you. The parts you cannot see are still there, but hidden. Cats often hunt at night, and this moonlit background adds suspense to the picture. The moon is the light source, so put it in before you colour the cat to see where to shade and highlight the fur.

The eyes are fixed on its prey.

The whole position forms an S-shape.

Use bluish highlights, as the moon casts a cold, eerie light.

The cat would look like this from the side.

Draw in the slope when you do the basic shapes, as it affects the way the legs are positioned.

The top of the head is flatter where it touches the floor.

For the cat's fur, do tiny strokes in darker pencil when the base colour is dry.

Rolling

Cats often roll over like this when they feel contented and safe. Here, the whole body is limp and relaxed, so make the lines fluid and soft to give a gentle feel. Although you are seeing the cat upside-down, draw it without turning the paper around. Do a fluffy rug as a background to add to the peaceful atmosphere.

The cat's tummy is exposed to the light, so make it paler.

Different kinds of domestic cat

There are lots of different breeds of domestic or pet cat. They are all basically alike in build, but here you can see some important differences to watch out for when drawing specific types.

Domestic shorthairs

Many of the pet cats you see around are of this type, though they may not be pure-bred. Domestic shorthairs are solid and chunky with close, thick fur. They have rounded heads and bodies set on short, sturdy legs, and are bred in a huge range of colours. This one is a tortoiseshell. To colour it, follow the tips on page 10.

The eyes are very round and a deep copper colour.

The paws and tail-tip are blunt.

Oriental shorthairs

These cats also have short fur, but they are sleeker, slimmer and have longer limbs, muzzles and tails than domestic shorthairs. There are several distinct breeds, one of the most popular being the Siamese.

You can tell a Siamese by its pale body and darker face, legs and tail, which are called its points. One way to draw Siamese markings is with thick paper and watercolours. Dampen the paper slightly, then apply a very light grey or fawn wash. When this is nearly dry, add the darker points.

Use pinky-grey for the points of this lilac-point Siamese.

The eyes are a vivid blue.

The head is wedge-shaped, with a longish muzzle.

The paint will spread, or "bleed", a bit, so apply it over a smaller area than you actually need. For a soft, realistic look, dab it with a tissue to blend the edges into the wash.

This is a seal-point Siamese.

Pale fawn base.

Dark-brown points.

Rex cats

The body is slender and set on long, slim legs.

The tail is long, very thin and pointed.

The whiskers are very long and curved.

This unusual-looking breed has a silky, curly coat which grows in rippling waves. To draw this effect, it is best to use coloured pencils, which make it easier to control your lines. Use a paler colour for the base, then build up the darker shades on top in rows of short, curved lines to create a ridged look.

The paws are small and oval.

Longhaired cats

When drawing a longhaired cat like this smoke Persian, remember that under all its fur, its body is like any other cat's. So start with the basic shapes, but notice that in this breed, the head is a bit bigger in relation to the rest of the body.

For the smoke colour, apply a silver-grey base. Add streaks of darker grey along the back. Blend these with black on the face, legs and tail. Use the lines of the fur to give shape to the body.*

Even in profile, these cats have such short noses that their heads fit easily into a circle.

Tiny ears

The legs are short and strong.

The fur grows in a long ruff around the neck and chest.

The body is solid and thickset.

The tail is very plumy.

There is more about drawing long, short and curly fur on page 8.

Kittens and cubs

Kittens make lovely, lively pictures. They are quite hard to draw, though, because their bodies are softer with less definite lines than adult cats'. They also have different proportions.

Four-week-old kitten

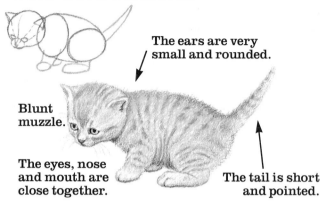

The ears are very small and rounded.

Blunt muzzle.

The eyes, nose and mouth are close together.

The tail is short and pointed.

Very young kittens like these have big heads in relation to their bodies.* Their legs are quite short and thick, with big paws. Kittens look cuddly as their fur is very soft. For a fluffy look, blur the outlines a bit so there are no hard edges.

Nine-week-old kitten

At this age, the ears are quite long and pointed.

The basic body shapes are very round.

A nursing cat and kittens

The cat and kittens form a fan-shape.

The kittens' heads and bodies overlap. The legs and paws are tucked away out of sight.

The wriggling tails add a lively touch.

The closed eyes give the cat a contented look.

For this grouping, position the mother cat before starting on the kittens. Use her front and back legs to help you put each kitten in the right place.

Use smooth, flowing lines to create a peaceful feeling. Notice how the cat's body is long and loose, while the kittens are rounded and tightly packed together.

Their different colours and markings also add interest. For each one, do the palest colours first, then the patches and stripes. For a soft look, use light strokes.

Compare these kittens' proportions with the adult cat on page 4.

Kittens at play

Kittens are bundles of energy and love playing. In the pictures below, look at how much movement and mood come from the paws, legs and tails.

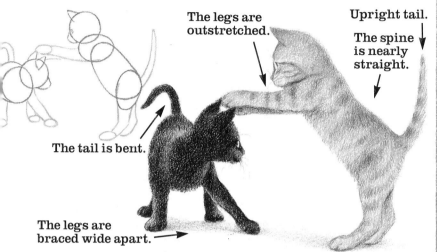

The legs are outstretched.

Upright tail.

The spine is nearly straight.

The tail is bent.

The legs are braced wide apart.

Draw the black kitten first. It is seen from the front, so you need to use foreshortening (page 11) to get it right. Its body is low and tense, ready to spring.

To position the ginger kitten, look at the space between the two animals. The ginger one's body is parallel with the line of the other's left foreleg.

Its eye is fixed on the ball.

There is a smooth curve from the spine to the tail-tip.

For this crouching position, draw the head and body shapes close together. Make the tabby stripes crinkly to give the body a compressed, coiled look.

The taut whiskers and flicked-up tail give the kitten a cheeky, playful air.

Cubs

Like domestic kittens, baby wild cats, often called cubs, look different from adults. Compare these two with the adult ones on page 21.

Lynx cub

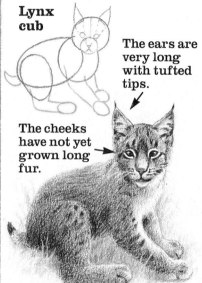

The ears are very long with tufted tips.

The cheeks have not yet grown long fur.

The huge legs and paws make the cub look gawky.

Cheetah cub

The head and face are more rounded than the adult's.

There is a long ridge of silvery hair here.

The coat is fluffy.

Wild cats

With their dramatic markings and powerful, elegant bodies, wild cats* make striking drawings. Though their size and colouring make them seem very different from pet cats, in fact they have a similar body structure.

Drawing heads

Use the construction method on page 6, but alter the shapes as shown to make these heads quite different.

European wild cat

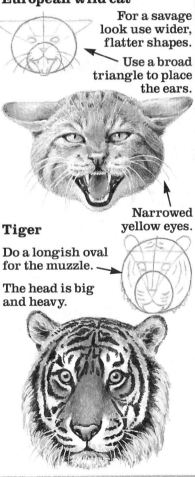

For a savage look use wider, flatter shapes.

Use a broad triangle to place the ears.

Narrowed yellow eyes.

Tiger

Do a longish oval for the muzzle.

The head is big and heavy.

Tiger

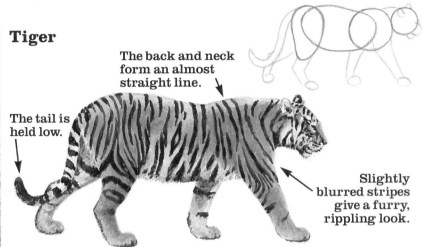

The back and neck form an almost straight line.

The tail is held low.

Slightly blurred stripes give a furry, rippling look.

The tiger is the biggest of all cats. It has a heavy head (see left) and body set on thick, strong legs. Try painting it with pale yellow-brown watercolour. Let this dry, then add red-brown as shown. While this is still damp, paint in the black stripes.

Serval

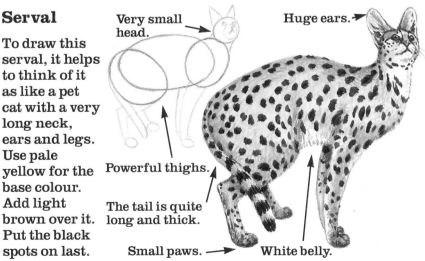

Very small head.

Huge ears.

Powerful thighs.

The tail is quite long and thick.

Small paws.

White belly.

To draw this serval, it helps to think of it as like a pet cat with a very long neck, ears and legs. Use pale yellow for the base colour. Add light brown over it. Put the black spots on last.

20

*Very large wild cats, such as lions (see pages 22-23), tigers and cheetahs, are known as big cats.

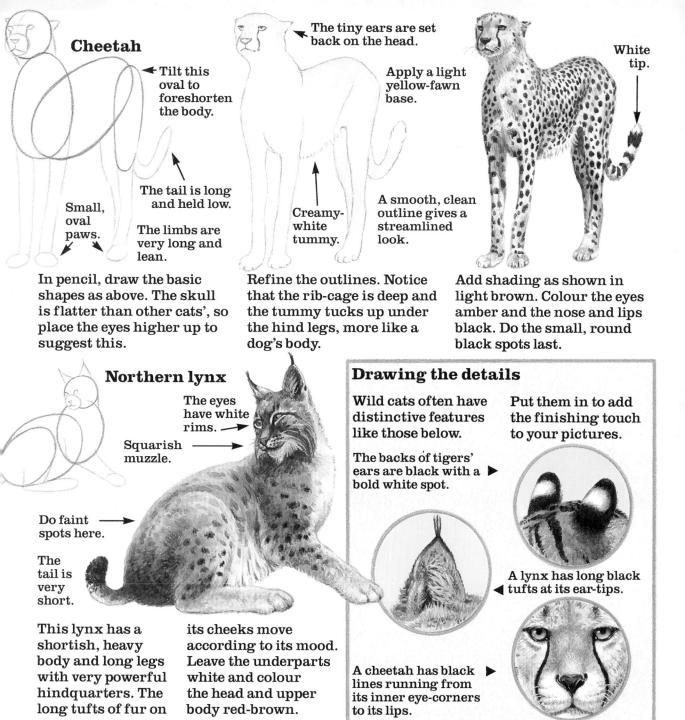

Cheetah

Tilt this oval to foreshorten the body.

Small, oval paws.

The tail is long and held low.

The limbs are very long and lean.

In pencil, draw the basic shapes as above. The skull is flatter than other cats', so place the eyes higher up to suggest this.

The tiny ears are set back on the head.

Apply a light yellow-fawn base.

Creamy-white tummy.

A smooth, clean outline gives a streamlined look.

Refine the outlines. Notice that the rib-cage is deep and the tummy tucks up under the hind legs, more like a dog's body.

White tip.

Add shading as shown in light brown. Colour the eyes amber and the nose and lips black. Do the small, round black spots last.

Northern lynx

The eyes have white rims.

Squarish muzzle.

Do faint spots here.

The tail is very short.

This lynx has a shortish, heavy body and long legs with very powerful hindquarters. The long tufts of fur on its cheeks move according to its mood. Leave the underparts white and colour the head and upper body red-brown.

Drawing the details

Wild cats often have distinctive features like those below.

Put them in to add the finishing touch to your pictures.

The backs of tigers' ears are black with a bold white spot. ▶

A lynx has long black tufts at its ear-tips. ◀

A cheetah has black lines running from its inner eye-corners to its lips. ▶

21

A pride of lions

Unlike most wild cats, lions live in groups, or prides, instead of alone. Here is a scene to copy. Opposite and below are suggestions for how to go about it, together with tips on drawing the lions' basic shapes.

A clear blue sky adds a feeling of heat. Do a pale blue base, then blend in darker blue pencil at the top.

Use a light sandy-fawn as the base for the landscape. Add warm oranges and browns over it.

The mountains in the distance frame the scene and give it a sense of scale. Do them in light violet, as colours look paler and bluer the further away they are.

Dark spots here.

The lions' tails add movement to the scene and guide the eye from one part to the next.

The three cubs form a roughly triangular shape.

This lioness and the seated one opposite face into the middle, which helps to frame the picture and focus your eyes on it.

Do the rich brown mane last, over a sandy base.

In real life this lion would be bigger than the lionesses, but you should draw him smaller here as he is further away.

The three lions in the middle are looking straight at you, giving the picture a strong focus.

22

How to copy the scene

In pencil, sketch in the line of the horizon. Then do the lioness nearest the front on the left. You can position and size up the rest in relation to her.* When you have drawn the whole scene, colour it in using the tips below. Work on the landscape and lions at the same time, so all the different colours are balanced and don't clash or merge together too much.

This young adult male's mane is not fully grown.

For the lions, use a pale sandy base with a mixture of gold and red-brown on top. Leave the chins white.

The way this lioness's head overlaps the young male helps to connect the two distant lions to the rest of the scene.

The basic shapes

Lions and lionesses have long muzzles, big heads and thick, powerful bodies.

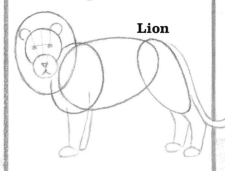

Lion

Use similar shapes as for a tiger (see page 20), but with bigger, rounder ears and an outer oval for the mane.

Lioness

Seen from the side, this lioness's body and legs form a triangle.

Squarish muzzle.

Cub

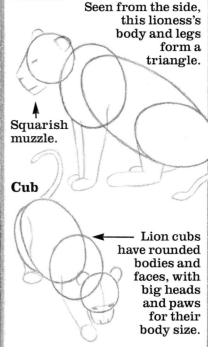

Lion cubs have rounded bodies and faces, with big heads and paws for their body size.

*There is more advice about arranging a picture on page 30.

Cartoon cats

Cats' strong characters, expressive faces and bodies and their habit of getting into comic scrapes as they roam make them ideal subjects for cartoons. Below and on the next three pages you can see how to draw cats in a cartoon style to make lively, funny pictures full of interest and action.

Cartoon cat

In pencil, start by doing the basic shapes as shown above. To get a comic look, exaggerate features like the eyes, teeth and claws and use strong, bold lines.

Zigzags make the outline look soft and fluffy.

Go over the outlines and features in waterproof black felt tip pen*, then lightly pencil in the inner edges of the markings. Try to keep all the lines clear and clean.

Leave the white markings blank and apply a base in light orange over the rest. When this dries, put in the stripes in darker orange. Use bright, solid colours to get a lively look: felt tips or coloured inks work best.

Add a bent whisker and a few stray hairs last, in black, to give the cat more character.

Colour the eyes bright green when you have done the markings. Add tiny black pupils when the green is dry.

A collar and name tag add a touch of extra colour and fun.

Give each marking a definite, crisp edge for a more striking effect. White patches on a bright coat make the cat look clownish.

24

*You could use ink to outline your finished drawing, but a felt tip is quicker and easier and gives a good strong line.

Cartooning different kinds of cat

Fat cat

Very round, big face and body.

Broad, coloured patches on a white coat help to make the cat look fat.

Big paws

Wide legs

Thin cat

A curved body and tail look slinky.

Make the basic face shape like a leaf for an exotic look.

Bright blue eyes.

Colouring the legs and tail in dark grey makes them look slim and creates Siamese markings.

Longhaired cat

Do the face and body as semi-circles.

To give the impression of long, flowing fur, do looped lines hanging from the tail and the backs of the legs.

Add tufts on the tips of the ears.

Kittens

Spiky whiskers give a lively look.

Short, stiff, pointed tail.

For this tabby colour, use light brown as a base. When it is dry, add the stripes in dark brown pencil, ink or felt tip.

Tiny movement lines add energy and action.

25

Cat characters

It is fun and good practice to try cartooning different cat characters. Below are a few to copy. Notice how you can completely alter the cat's expression and character just by changing details like the head shape.

Alley cat

A nick at the edge of one ear suggests the cat has been in a fight.

Make the whiskers bent and ragged.

A fish skeleton shows the cat has been scavenging through dustbins.

A big grin gives a jaunty air.

Put in the occasional zigzag for a scruffy look.

Sly cat

A pointed, diamond-shaped face gives a cunning air.

Slanting eyes.

Do Siamese markings.* The dark-brown "mask" makes the cat look more sinister.

A long, low body makes the cat look sneaky.

Big "wicked" grin.

Smug cat

Set the eyes high up the face so the cat seems to be looking down its nose.

Draw the eyelids half-closed.

A small, neat smile gives a smug look.

Upturned whiskers increase the snooty expression.

Pale blue shading makes the white look crisp and clean.

Scaredy cat

Zigzag ridges on the back look like raised fur.

Make the eyes wide. Add the black pupils when the yellow base is dry.

Jagged black and white patches add to the spiky, tense feel.

26   *See page 25.

Comic cat capers

When you do comic sequences like those below, keep the backgrounds fairly plain and simple, so they don't distract from what is going on in the cartoon.

Falling cat

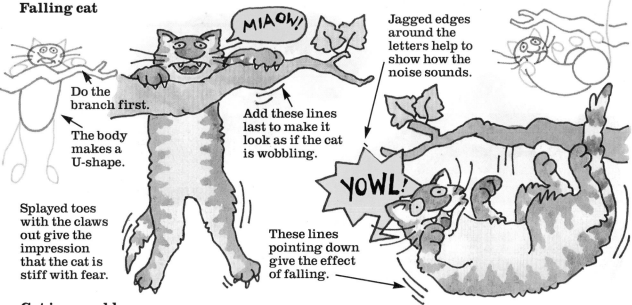

Do the branch first.

The body makes a U-shape.

MIAOW!

Jagged edges around the letters help to show how the noise sounds.

Add these lines last to make it look as if the cat is wobbling.

Splayed toes with the claws out give the impression that the cat is stiff with fear.

YOWL!

These lines pointing down give the effect of falling.

Cat in a cauldron

This strip cartoon is based on the idea that cats have nine lives and so can survive almost any mishap. Sketch out the strip in pencil, starting with the boxes. Use a ruler to make sure all the frames are even.

In each frame, do the cat first, then the main objects like the broom. Add the witch, then the sound effects and finishing touches like the movement lines, bubbles, steam and splashes of potion.

YOWL!

HEE! HEE!!

Legendary cats

Throughout history, cats have been both feared and worshipped by people all over the world. Here are a few which have made their mark.

Bast

The Ancient Egyptians were some of the first people known to have kept pet cats. They believed the animals were sacred, and worshipped a cat goddess called Bast or Bastet. She was the goddess of life and was also associated with light, music and pleasure.

Use a rich rust-red to suggest that the statue is made of clay or pottery.

Elbows on this line.

Dividing the basic L-shape roughly into thirds like this may help you get the proportions right.

Lines parallel with the front of the base help keep the kittens in perspective.

We know about Bast from old Egyptian paintings and statues like the one on the left. She was usually shown as an elegant, slim woman with a cat's head. To draw this statue, start with a three-dimensional L-shape for the basic figure. Add the head and arms as shown. Refine the outlines and fill in the details before colouring the picture.

This is a musical instrument called a sistrum.

Black cats

Colour the eyes in a brilliant copper.

Black cats are symbols of good luck in some places, but they have also been traditionally linked with witchcraft and the Devil.

Sabre-toothed tiger

This big cat, also known as Smilodon, lived millions of years ago in prehistoric times and is now extinct. It was only distantly related to the tigers of today, and in fact probably looked more like a lion. It had a massive, powerful body and huge jaws spiked with 15cm (6in) fangs to kill its prey.

Try tracing this sabre-toothed tiger, or build it up using the same basic shapes as for a lioness.*

Add the fangs last, in white.

Make the tail a bit like a lynx's.

Colour the fur tawny like a lion, with a pale belly.

This mixed view is probably because their jet-black fur and glowing eyes look especially beautiful but also a bit sinister and mysterious. To get a rich, gleaming black, use a grey, dark blue or violet base. Leave this to show through where there are highlights. Gradually deepen the colour on the darker parts with black pencil or paint. For the blackest shadows, do the strokes very close together.

Use the tips on page 15 to help you with this position and the eerie moonlit background.

*See pages 22-23.

Making your pictures work

Good pictures involve more than just drawing convincing likenesses. Here are tips about four elements which add a lot of impact to a picture.

Composition

Roughly sketch the whole triangle first, then work out each kitten's place in it before putting in the details.

The composition of a picture means the way all the things in it are arranged. Here are two ways to group four kittens into a good composition. In the picture above, the kittens form a triangle. The grouping is interesting because the kittens look so alike but are on slightly different levels. The triangle shape draws your eye from left to right across each face.

This grouping also works well because it is nearly symmetrical: if you folded it vertically down the middle, each half would almost mirror the other. ⟶

A good way to compose a picture is to sketch each thing you want to include on a separate scrap of paper. Move the bits around until they look right together.

Point of view

The angle or point of view from which you draw can add power to a scene. This prowling kitten is seen from its own eye-level, making a dramatic picture as you look straight into its stare.

The blades of grass show how small the kitten is: its tail hardly comes above them.

Draw the kitten first. Its body is hidden because of foreshortening, so make the face detailed as it is the focus of attention. Put the grass and flowers in last.

Light and dark

Do a pale yellowy-white base for the fur, then build up the shading in tawny brown. Add the dark spots on top.

The lines of the leopard's back and tummy echo the curves of the branches above and below it.

The spots and stripes of wild cats like this leopard are not just decorative, but help to hide or camouflage them.

Light and shadow help to give shape and colour to things (see pages 5 and 8). They also add contrast and mood to a picture and stop it looking flat and dull. Here, the dappled shadows cast by the light falling through the leaves blend in with the leopard's spotted coat and make an eye-catching scene. Draw the branches and leaves first, as the leopard's position is shaped by what it is lying on. To colour the scene, first note the light source, which is sunshine from above. This and the foliage affect where you need to shade the fur.

Backgrounds

Putting a background in a picture stops the main image "floating" on the page and adds atmosphere. It can also help to focus your eye on the cat (see page 12). In this case, it brings out the cats' shapes and colours by echoing them.

For this scene, sketch in the lines of the sofa to help you judge where to put the cats. Draw them in, making them quite detailed so they stand out. Use loose blotches for the flowered pattern so it is not too distracting.

As the cats are facing left, place them slightly to the right of the picture to balance it properly.

The flowers echo the round, blooming faces of these Persian cats.

Index

Chris Chapman is represented by Maggie Mundy Agency.

First published in 1991 by Usborne Publishing Ltd, Usborne House, 83-85 Saffron Hill, London EC1N 8RT.

Copyright © Usborne Publishing Ltd, 1991

The name Usborne and the device 🎈 are Trade Marks of Usborne Publishing Ltd.

Printed in Belgium.